T0146904

The Adventures of SPIKE the Cat

Robert J. Morrissey

iUniverse

THE ADVENTURES OF SPIKE THE CAT

iUniverse books may be ordered through booksellers or by contacting:

iUniverse
1663 Liberty Drive
Bloomington, IN 47403
www.iuniverse.com
1-800-Authors (1-800-288-4677)

Because of the dynamic nature of the Internet, any web addresses or links contained in this book may have changed since publication and may no longer be valid. The views expressed in this work are solely those of the author and do not necessarily reflect the views of the publisher, and the publisher hereby disclaims any responsibility for them.

Any people depicted in stock imagery provided by Thinkstock are models, and such images are being used for illustrative purposes only. Certain stock imagery © Thinkstock.

ISBN: 978-1-5320-2708-6 (sc)
ISBN: 978-1-5320-2709-3 (hc)
ISBN: 978-1-5320-2710-9 (e)

Print information available on the last page.

iUniverse rev. date: 07/14/2017

To my dear children:

Karen, Lynn, Bob and Jodi

Dad

The Adventures of Spike the Cat

Spike is an ordinary tiger cat. He's really no different than any other house cat, except for the circumstances of his birth and the effects these had on him. In order to understand Spike, you must know these circumstances.

It was a dark and stormy night. The wind was blowing ...

"Spike, stay away from the computer."

Hi, dear reader, it's me, Spike. Bob is looking for me in the other room, but ow, ow, meow, I escaped and sneaked back here.

Sorry about that. Let me begin again, with a bit more manners.

It was a dark and stormy night ...

"Spike, I'm trying to write your life story. Would you please stay away from the computer?"

Excuse me for a moment, dear reader. Spike is having a problem. He's being a cat and not listening. I'll put him out and be right back.

"Spike, come here!"

Hi, dear reader, it's me, Spike. Bob is looking for me in the other room, but *ow, ow, meow,* I escaped and sneaked back here.

I just want to quickly tell you that he has written my story before, but let's face it— the guy means well, but the world's greatest writer he ain't.

To begin with, it wasn't a dark and stormy night at all. It was a beautiful starlit night in the springtime. My mom was preparing to give birth to my brothers and sisters and me. Like any cat about to become a mother, she wanted to be left alone, but didn't want to skimp on comfort, so of course, she found a nice, secluded spot in the family car.

Well, wouldn't you know it, at about 3:00 a.m., Sue (that's Bob's wife) decides to have a baby, too. She gets in the family car at three o'clock in the morning to mosey on over to the maternity ward at the hospital. Now, personally, I don't see why she couldn't have her baby in the car like my mom, but that's humans, I guess. Always doing things the hard way.

Anyway, Sue and Bob (and their expected baby) pile into the car and away we go.

I'm not going to go into detail about the trip. I don't remember it, of course, since I hadn't been born yet. But from everything I've been told, the police made a full report and have it on file, if you're interested. Apparently, Bob was driving far too fast while Sue screamed at him to go even faster.

We arrived at the hospital surrounded by police cars, and in plenty of time for all of us. During the wild ride, however, Mom discovered Sue had a bag of nice soft things, and since they smelled much nicer than the soiled spot under the car seat, she climbed right in and prepared for the big moment.

At the hospital, a very nice nurse loaded Sue and her bag into a wheelchair and raced her straight to the maternity ward. Now, it's only natural to think that Bob would have joined her, but he was taken straight to the emergency room and sedated. That means he was given a shot to calm him down. I guess Bob was now screaming about the baby coming, too.

Humans. I just don't know about them sometimes.

In the meantime, Mom, still in Sue's bag, arrived at the maternity ward. The nurses put

Sue in bed and tossed the bag on the floor, where it got pushed under the bed and out of the way.

Well, it wasn't long before Sue goes into final labor, Mom goes into final labor and—WHAMO!—all of a sudden, there was a Charley, and me, and my two brothers and two sisters. Oh, Charley is Sue's baby. And would you believe it? Charley and I were born at the exact same moment. It all happened so quick they never had a chance to move Sue into the delivery room. The doctor just picked up Charley right there and gave him a whack on the behind and Charley let out a big MEEEOOOWWW, just like that.

The doc almost dropped Charley, but he

recovered just in time to hear him give out a big WAAAHHH! No problem!

I'll explain it to you, but if you insist on thinking like a human, forget it. You'll never understand. If you're a cat, you'll understand perfectly.

You see, we cats are a lot smarter than you humans think we are. In fact, we're so smart (please check to make sure no adult is reading this), we can talk.

Not all of us, mind you. Not even very many of us. But I'm one of those that can. When you think about it, there really isn't much need for cats to talk anyway. We get everything we need without talking, and so much of what humans say is just gibberish.

Talking about the weather? Boring! We all know the weather just by looking outside. Asking what's for dinner? Does it matter? You should eat it anyway because it's better than starving.

Now, where was I? Oh, yes, Charley. Well, since Charley and I were born at the exact same moment, the signals got crossed. This means that Charley can speak cat and human, and I can speak human and cat. The amazing thing isn't my being able to speak human. I've already spoken human in a past life. I've already said we cats are smart. It's that Charley can speak "Catonese," or cat language. As far as I know, no humans have ever been smart enough to do that.

You have a problem with this, right? I'm sure plenty of humans would, but look at it this way: you're reading this, right? And I wrote this, right? Then, you and I are talking, right? No problem!

Wait, there's still a problem? Sheesh! Stop thinking like a human. Take my word for it, and let me get on with the story. Bob will be back soon, and he doesn't like me using his computer. He says my fur keeps getting on the keyboard and gumming up the works.

Anyway, I never had a problem with being able to talk. That's because hardly anybody knows about it. I only talk to humans I trust, like Charley and Bob, and now you. Why you? Because I know you love cats. How do

I know? You're reading this book, and this book was written by a cat, therefore you love cats. Charley, however, had some real problems because he spoke cat. Lucky for him, he also got the ability to think like a cat, which makes him fast on his feet. That kept him out of trouble because I was able to explain everything to him before he let the dog out of the bag. (I know you humans say, "Let the cat out of the bag," but that's a big mistake. If we cats happen to find ourselves in a bag, we are perfectly capable of letting ourselves out, even shredding the bag if we have to. Dogs, on the other hand, aren't so smart, and it's usually necessary for someone to show them the way out.)

Now, please, no more interruptions! I was going to tell you about solving Charley's cat-talk problem. Well, for the first couple days, nothing much happened. Then Mom and her litter were discovered under the bed. You'd think somebody declared World War VII or something. The nurses were freaking out that there was a cat and kittens under the bed. A perfectly normal, everyday thing, right? Not to her. The nurse grabbed a bag (there's that bag again, as if we couldn't get out) and was going to ship us out and put us up for adoption! Fortunately, by this time, Bob was in control of himself and in the room with Sue and Charley. As soon as he saw us and the ruckus the nurse was making, he took us all home. Oh, no, he didn't take us all home.

Just us cats. Charley, being a human baby, had to stay in the hospital with Sue for a few days. See what I mean? Already my brothers and sisters and I are starting to take care of ourselves, but Sue and Charley have to stay behind for some training or something. Sheesh! We cats really are smart.

But that doesn't matter now, I guess. A few days later, Sue brought Charley home and we were a family. That's where the real adventure begins.

Hmmmm! That's a pretty good chapter ending, and if this were a long book I might make the next part Chapter Two, but since Bob will get tired of looking for me soon,

I won't have enough time to write a book. That's why it isn't Chapter Two.

NOT CHAPTER TWO

As I was just a kitten, I didn't have a lot of experience dealing with humans, so I had a few minor problems, at first. The first time I got hungry, which was right away, I didn't say "Meow" or "Mew," I said "Wah!" That's right, I went straight to baby talk. Well, that's just not done among us cats. Mom explained to me that I would have to behave like a cat, and start right now. Mom was kind of set her in ways, but she was Mom, so I listened.

For a while anyway, but more on that later.

After a couple of days, Bob brought Sue and

Charley home. By that time, my brothers and sisters and I knew exactly where everything was, and we knew exactly what to do to get it. I don't mean to say we didn't need help. Of course we did. We were only a few days old! But we were way ahead of poor Charley. When we were hungry, we crawled over to Mom to get fed. Charley just stayed there and screamed his head off. I think it's the way we were raised. Mom seldom left us alone, so she was always there around chow time. But Sue was always off doing other things. She just couldn't get the hang of it. She'd leave Charley in a cage-like thing called a crib and go away, sometimes for a whole hour. The poor kid would wake up hungry and Wow!, you should have heard the ruckus.

He was louder than all us cats put together. We'd bury our heads into Mom's fur belly, but you could still hear him.

Charley did have his own room, though, which was kind of nice. We slept in the corner of the kitchen. The only nice thing was that we got to sleep with Mom right from the start, nuzzled up against her.

After a few weeks, my brothers and sisters and I were really into taking care of ourselves, but Charley was still crying "Wah!" every time he wanted food or to have his diaper changed. We didn't need diapers. We had a newspaper for a while, and then Mom showed up with this nice box of sand, and we knew exactly what to do. No problem!

Every once in a while, Sue brought Charley down to the kitchen to see the "itty bitty kitties." That was us, by the way. How insulting! I mean, we were the ones taking care of ourselves, not Charley. Who was "itty bitty" now? Still, I didn't say anything because Mom wouldn't let me talk human.

I guess as far as humans go, Charley was a good-looking kid. He didn't have much hair, but I could see he was working on it. He had little sprouts here and there, but certainly wasn't fully equipped with fur like us. It kept us warm when it was cold, and cool when it was hot. Charley was always being put in new clothes depending on the temperature outside. You humans are too much work!

Anyway, one time when Sue brought Charley down, she put him on a blanket on the floor while she went to check on something called "formula." Yuck! I got a taste of it once when she wasn't looking. I was expecting mother's milk, but this was just powder and water. I guess it wasn't all that bad if it gave Charley what he needed, but it was nothing like mother's milk. So, when Sue left the room, I ran over to have a few words with Charley. We hadn't had a chance to talk since the hospital.

"Hi, Charley. Remember me?" I said. "I'm Spike, from the hospital."

"Ga ga goo goo," he said. That might not

be an exact quote because he really only spoke gibberish, but it's close enough.

I immediately switched to Catonese. No problem! He picked it up right away. I was afraid that he had forgotten it in the weeks we were separated, but not Charley.

"Hi, Spike," he said. "I like your name. Who gave it to you?"

"Your dad," I said. "He named all us kittens. But look, we don't have much time before your mom gets back. Just wanted to check in and see how things are going with you."

"Okay, I guess. I really don't have much experience to compare things to, but I can't complain. How are you making out?"

"Well, that's what I wanted to talk with you about. You see, I heard your mom and dad talking about finding a new home for us cats, and I kind of like it here. Besides, you and me being born at the same time and being able to talk to each other is important, right?"

"Yeah, I guess so," he said. I could have used more enthusiasm from Charley here, but the only thing he ever got enthusiastic about was his 'formula'. Yuck!

"I'm glad you agree," I said, hoping to completely convince him. "So, here's what we do. I'm going to go back to the edge of your blanket and act kind of cute. You point to me and say 'Kitty,' or something cute like that. We work this right, and they'll have to keep me. Okay?"

"No problem," he said. Again, I really could use more enthusiasm from this kid.

"Now you've got it!" I said, lying through my sharp teeth, but hoping for the best. I figured as a human, Charley could use all the encouragement he could get. "We're going to get along just fine."

I still had my doubts about Charley, but what could I say? He was my best human friend. After all, we understood each other!

I got back to the edge of the blanket just in time. I say "just in time" because humans don't always understand the ways of cats. They have some awful stories about cats getting too close to babies and sucking the breath out of them. Ridiculous. There's plenty of air for all of us. I don't know how such stories get started. Even if we could, we would never do such a thing—not to a baby. I'd also like to mention here that I never heard of a cat polluting the air. Only humans do that.

Now, back to our story. I bet you're wondering if Charley pulled it off. Well, Charley's mom came in, and I got set up in my cutest pose, eyes wide open and paws up. I was adorable. I mean, I was super cuddly. And in the most kittenish voice I could come up with I said, "Mew."

I got set up in my cutest pose, eyes wide open and paws up. I was adorable. I mean, I was super cuddly. And in the most kittenish voice I could come up with I said, "Mew."

Charley's head kind of jerked all over the place and he said, "Goo." He called me Goo! Ho boy, oh boy, oh boy, this is going to be tougher than I thought. And Charley sure wasn't helping because he looked at me and called me "Goo" again.

Ugh!

I mean, "Mew."

Fortunately, the one thing you can always say about humans is you never know what they're going to do next. While Charley's calling me "Goo," Sue called in Bob and told him he said, "Kitty, kitty." And he believed her. It was that simple. All that planning, and all the kid had to do was say, "Goo."

Soon, my brothers and sisters were living somewhere else, but Mom and I continued living with the Maxwells.

Like I said at the end of Not Chapter One, we were a family now.

NOT CHAPTER THREE

It was eight years ago that we became the family we are today. They were happy years, though there were some sad times, too. It took me a long time to get over Mom's death. At least it was a peaceful death, after a happy and healthy life. She just went to sleep and didn't wake up. I still miss her, but I know she's out there somewhere, probably even happier now than she was with us.

But now, on to happier memories. Let me tell you about the time Bob found out I could talk. It was two years ago. Sue was out shopping, and Bob had gone down to the school-bus stop to meet Charley. It was a beautiful fall day, and Charley was just beginning first grade. He passed kindergarten with honors, naturally, because he thought like a cat. This meant he thought faster, learned to read faster, do his math problems faster, and he was great at shapes. It was always a big occasion when Charley arrived home from school—big enough that I always met him at the door.

"Hi, Charley, how was school today?" I asked, running across the living-room carpet. Mom taught me to look before I spoke, and I always did. Except once, when I forgot. But Sue couldn't hear me over the dishwasher, and so she never knew. Oh, and one other time.

That day when Charley came home from school.

Bob just stood there, mouth hanging open and a real weird look on his face. I guess I'd describe it as a bulging eyes with a hand on his forehead. Charley was right behind him with a big grin on his face. Well, I guess I let the dog out of the bag.

"Spike can talk, Daddy," said Charley.

Bob looked at me kind of funny. If he had a cross or a stake like in Dracula, I think he would have held it out in front of him, or tried to stab me in the heart.

"Take it easy," I said.

"It's no big deal. Plenty of cats can talk. Now, sit down before you fall down, and I'll explain it to you."

Bob just stood there, mouth hanging open and a real weird look on his face. I guess I'd describe it as a bulging eyes with a hand on his forehead. Charley was right behind him with a big grin on his face.

And so, I explained it to him just like I explained it to you, but Bob didn't believe me. Here I am, talking to the guy, and he's saying it's not true. Can you believe that?

How dumb can you be? He even told me to stop talking because it wasn't right. Yes, he told someone he doesn't believe can talk to stop talking. Sheesh!

"Daddy," said Charley, "if you can't believe it, then just accept it." Now, that's Charley for you—good cat sense. The kid should be in college.

Well, that was then. Today, Bob talks to me all the time. Sue caught him talking to me a couple of times, but she just thinks he's crazy. At first, she thought it was cute, but that wore off after a while and our conversations got deeper. He wasn't just saying, "Here, kitty kitty." He was talking to me about work and sports and everything else, and she just thought he'd finally gone off the deep end. We never let her in on it, by the way. Sue is a nice person, but she gets excited if things aren't just right, and we decided it was best this way.

Now, let me tell you about some of the things that have happened to us over the years. There was the time I caught a cat burglar. Yeah, I know. It's ironic that a cat caught a cat burglar. That was ...

"Spike, get away from that computer! If I told you once, I've told you a thousand times, don't go near my computer."

Uh-oh, gotta go. I'll tell you later.

Now, let me see. Where was I before Spike got involved in my story. Oh, yes.

It was a dark and stormy night ...

Spike the Cat and the Symphony

*I*t was a dark and stormy night ...

"Honey," said Sue, "the Martins have invited us to the symphony Saturday night. Are you interested in going?"

"Oh, I don't know, sweetheart. I'm really enjoying writing my book. I'd like to go, but

when I get these flashes of creativity, I hate to stop writing."

"Okay, dear. Al isn't going to wear a tie, so you can be comfortable in your turtleneck. No need to dress up."

"You already said yes, didn't you?"

Hi, guys, it's me, Spike. What? Spike the Cat. Didn't you read the book title? Yes, that Spike the Cat. Okay, now that you remember me, I'll tell you this story before Bob gets back. He went to check on his clothes for the symphony. I was having a nice siesta, or cat nap, but when I heard them talking about the symphony, I remembered a story about the time I was asked to play in the symphony. What? Oh, yes, I'm quite talented, you know.

My instrument was the violin, but I gave that up when I noticed one of my relatives being used as a string. Catgut string is just a terrible invention! It's every cat's worst nightmare that they'll end up on a violin. I bet you didn't know that. Well, I went to the local animal shelter, and the orchestra stopped using catgut string right away when they heard that a demon cat was after them. Unfortunately, I just couldn't go back to playing the violin after that. I didn't have the stomach for it, so I switched to the piano.

Now, I know most of the great composers: Beethoven, Bach, Katsuturian, Mozart. What? You've never heard of Katsuturian? Oh, he's that Russian guy who wrote songs. They don't spell his name that way anymore, but that's because his wife hated cats and bought a dog, so I stopped playing his music. Really, dogs? Such poor taste.

Let's see, back to the symphony. I have to begin my story back in the eighteenth century, when I used to pal around with a guy named Domenico Scarlatti. What? You've never heard of Scarlatti? He was that Italian guy who wrote songs. Anyway, back to my story ... What? Oh, the eighteenth century was back during the 1700s. Yeah, whiz kid, that was three hundred years ago. How old am I? That's none of your business, dog breath ... Oh, you mean how could I have been around in the 1700s? No problem. Cats

have nine lives.

Domenico Scarlatti and I were sitting around one afternoon in Madrid. The prince he worked for asked Dom to put together a song for a party he was throwing for his buddies.

Well, anyway, Dom and I were sitting

around one afternoon in Madrid. Where's

Madrid? It's the capital of Sp ... Hey, wait a second. Look it up. That's what Bob always says, and he should know—he's a teacher. Of course, he only tells other people to look it up when he doesn't know the answer himself. Now, no more interruptions. Back to my good friend, Domenico Scarlatti. The prince he worked for asked Dom to put together a song for a party he was throwing for his buddies. Dom usually worked with a harpsichord—that's the piano-looking thing that guys like Dracula and the Phantom of the Opera play. Most of them are falling apart nowadays, so somebody invented the pianoforte. What? The pianoforte is the full name of the piano. Piano means to play softly; a pianoforte is what you play softly on. Got that? Good.

So, Dom has a couple hundred of these things put together, and he decides to use one of them rather than write a new song. He was feeling pretty lazy that day. Well, I knew the prince would be pretty mad at Dom if he ever found out—and you and I know they always find out—so I said to Dom, "Hey, Dom, old buddy, howsabout I write you a song?"

"Spike, mi amico, thatsa good of you, but you donna know how to writa song. I'll justa use one ofa my olda ones."

"But if the prince finds out, he may send you back to Italy."

"Hmmm, maybe you righta. I like this job.

The pay is pretty good, and the work is easy. Whatta you got in mind?"

"Oh, I have an idea for a song that I'll write and then play, and you'll get all the credit for teaching a cat how to play the piano. You'll be famous, and I'll bet the prince will be so pleased, he might even give you a raise."

Dom and I immediately went to work on the song. I picked out the notes on the piano, and he wrote them down. Twenty minutes later, we had a masterpiece of music on paper. Of course, Dom took all the credit for it. Well, he had to. Who would believe a talking cat could write music? In those days, if something weird happened, it was the old "off with the head" or "burn the witch at the stake" bit. Dom and I were no dummies.

That night, the prince had all his buddies in for the big party. I spent the rest of the day grooming myself so I'd look real classy. By the time the party got going, I was looking good. Had a nice, shiny coat and everything. Not a hair was out of place, and my whiskers were as white as the powdered wigs men wore in those days. Even my claws were keen and sharp.

They were holding this shindig in the ballroom. Big place. Must have been five hundred people there, with a throne on one end, big windows that stretched almost from the floor to the ceiling, and chandeliers all lit brightly with candles. I have to admit, all that fire around my fur made me nervous. I'm so glad they invented electricity. What? They didn't invent electricity, they discovered it? Look, I was there with Ben Franklin when he invented it. In fact, I was the one who held the kite while he went looking for his house keys. The man was always losing things. Now, if you want to hear the rest of my story, button your lip.

All the guys at the ball were dressed in fancy suits, short pants, long stockings, long coats, and powdered wigs. Nothing comfortable like today, where you wear faded jeans, baggy T-shirts, and sneakers with your toes nearly hanging out. If you think the men looked like nerds, you should have seen the ladies. Hair piled a foot high on their heads, but the dresses—oh, you should have seen the dresses. You had to be there. The dresses reached all the way to the floor and had to be five or six feet wide at the bottom. There was no room to walk around without crashing into somebody else. I should know. I had the dumb idea to cut across the ballroom floor. Let me tell you, it was like being caught in a tent city during a tornado. The band started playing, and every skirt in the place started swishing back and forth like the agitator in a washing machine. I lit out of there and was halfway up the drapes when Dom came over and helped me out (or is it meowt?) of the place. He gallantly carried me in his arms across the floor until I was safe, although all these women came over and said what a beautiful cat I was. "Oh, isn't he precious?" and "Isn't he lovely?" They didn't even care they almost stepped all over me out there. I swear, humans never change.

I had the dumb idea to cut across the ballroom floor. Let me tell you, it was like being caught in a tent city during a tornado.

Anyway, the time came for the prince to announce that Dom had written a song just for this party and would now play it for everyone. Dom got up, bowed to the prince, and thanked him for allowing him to play, but he had a surprise for everyone: the cat who helped him write this song was going to play it on the pianoforte. The crowd was stunned. The prince was stunned. His buddies were stunned. *Oh, no,* I'm thinking, *it's off-with-his-head time!* But no, the prince smiled and told him to go on. So, Dom explained how we did it, and everyone was smiling and laughing. I couldn't believe it as I came out, took my bow, and jumped on the piano.

As I got ready to play, Dom went over to

the band. Actually, it wasn't a band like we have today. In fact, they didn't even call it a band—they called it a chamber orchestra. Just a bunch of violins and a big cello. Yes, a big cello. What? Oh, it rhymes with Jell-O, and it was so big, the musician could barely get his legs around it to hold it in place on the floor. Once Dom got them all tuned up and ready to go, he turned to me and said, "Shalla we begin, Spike? Tella me when you ara ready."

"Meow," I said, and off we went. All the guys playing violin started building up for my big introduction, the music getting faster and louder. I sat on the piano looking very professional, occasionally cleaning a spot off one of my toes, or running a paw through my fur, just to make sure I was still looking good. Then, the violins all quieted down. My time was almost here. Dom looked at me and nodded. I gingerly stepped out to the keyboard and began to play the *Cat's Fugue*.

The crowd went wild. Well, maybe not wild. Maybe they were moved. A little. Okay, so there was some polite applause, but at least they didn't throw rotten tomatoes! Anyway, if you want to check out my story, you can probably find it online, or you can ask your music teacher. Domenico Scarlatti may have his name on the song, but you and I know who wrote it, right?

Right.

Dom looked at me and nodded. I gingerly stepped out
to the keyboard and began to play the Cat's Fugue.

Spike the Cat Learns to Fly

I t was a dark and stormy night ...

"Spike, get off that computer and give me that candy. You get your own treats to eat."

Please excuse this interruption, dear reader, particularly at the beginning of *The World's Greatest Novel* (working title). Spike wants to write it, of course, but he's not going to—I am. He means well, but the world's greatest writer he ain't.

Now, where was I? Oh, yes ...

It was a dark and stormy night ...

"If you served better meals, I wouldn't eat your candy."

"Spike, I serve you the best cat food money can buy. I serve it on our best china, and by candlelight. What more do you want?"

"It's ... it's cat food. I don't want cat food. How would you like eating chicken guts and horse hooves for breakfast?"

"If I were a cat, I'd love it. After all, cats love cat food."

"Did you forget what your doctor said?"

"No, Spike, I remember perfectly well what she said. She said that if I didn't stop having these 'looney' conversations with you, she'd have me committed, so buzz off. Go away. You're just a fat tabby that can talk. That doesn't mean I have to talk to you."

"Look, Bob, you said we were going on a plane ride today. If you get stuck in that pre-primer book you're writing, we're not going on our trip."

"Okay, if you let me write this novel, I'll take you for a plane ride. Deal?"

"Okay, deal, but at the rate you're writing that novel, I'll have to use up six of my lives before I get that plane ride."

"Spike, please—puhleeze—get out of here. Look, there's hair on the keyboard. Just go away so I can work."

It was a dark ...

"You know, that's not very original. My litter box is filled with papers that begin 'It was a dark and stormy night ... ' Come on, Bob, let's go for a plane ride. Puhleeze?"

"Spike, you're the reason I can't fly. The doctor says I'm in great health and my vision is perfect. So, do you have any idea—even the faintest notion—as to why I can't fly a plane?"

"You talk to a cat?"

"Good. Now get out of here so I can stop talking to a cat!"

It was a dark and stormy night ...

Hi, it's me, Spike, again. Bob is a little frazzled right now and hasn't been able to type for two days. If only he could think like a cat, he'd stay nice and calm and sleep a whole lot more. Oh, well, that's life.

But you might be asking yourself, "Did you ever go for that plane ride?" Boy, is that a story! Let me tell you all about it.

The day after our spat, Bob had calmed down a bit. He was still a little jerky, but his eyes focused again. He told Sue that he had writer's block. That's like a baseball player who goes into a hitting slump. The only difference is that a hitter usually works out of his slump. With Bob, there was no chance. His best writing would be a slump for an illiterate termite. Besides, how could he be stuck? How can he not know what to write next? He's writing my life story, and he can't come up with another word when there's so much to tell? Just ask me what happened, and the story writes itself. I think this just proves my point. I mean, I like the guy, but a writer he ain't.

Fortunately, he is a pilot. A very good pilot.

In order to get his creative juices flowing and hopefully break his writer's block, I pushed him to go on the plane again. I told him that "going up in the plane again might clear the cobwebs," and he bought it hook, line, and sinker. Which reminds me of the time we went fishing. I caught the biggest fish ... oh, wait, this is the story about how I flew a plane. Let me get back to that.

Bob was eager to get to the airplane, and so he hopped in his car and took off. But ho, ho, ho, guess who was under the seat? Right—me.

By the time we got to the airport, he was really psyched and ready to go. He listened to the pilots talking to the control tower on his portable aircraft radio all the way to the airport. When we got close to the airplane garage (called a hangar), we could hear the air-traffic controllers talking to the pilots. Bob even made believe his car was an airplane and radioed in to the tower to let them know what he was doing. I can see why is doctor is worried about him. Maybe he is crazy.

Anyway, at the airport, while Bob unloaded his flight gear, like earphones, maps, and all sorts of metal and plastic stuff pilots use to figure things out, I slipped out of the car and slinked over (I'm a cat, what can I say? I have a way of being sneaky) to the hangar. I don't know why it's a called a hangar, though. It didn't see any planes hanging there. I also didn't see Bob's plane. It was parked somewhere in the middle of the garage ... err, I mean hangar. I guess in order to work at the airport, you had to be really good at puzzles because the planes were parked all over the floor, and not too neatly I might add. To find your plane, you had to be really good at mazes. I finally saw Bob's plane when they brought it out. They only had to move five other planes to get to it. Sheesh!

While Bob went into the office to get permission to use the sky or something, I found a nice, warm spot to take a sunbath. After all, if we're going to be closer to the sun, why not? Now, as I was getting comfortable, I heard Bob talking to a woman about the weather conditions aloft, so I looked up to the sky. Not a cloud in sight—bright, sunny, and warm—but this guy has to ask about the weather. Yep, humans.

I guess he was worried it might be a dark and stormy night after all.

Well, he finally came out of the office with all sorts of papers with funny figures on them, telling him the weather was bright, sunny, and warm. You know, the stuff I figured out by looking up. I hope he didn't have to pay for that.

By that time, his plane was on the apron. That's pilot talk for your plane is out there somewhere if you can find it, and please be careful not to bruise the other planes when you taxi out to the runway before takeoff.

He walked toward a beautiful white airplane with blue stripes, the wings on top, and everything else where it should be (I think). He put down his case and opened the door on the driver's side (I think). It's really hard to tell which is the driver's side because a plane has two of everything— two steering wheels, two sets of brakes, and no gas pedals. I just hoped all the dials and other gadgets made up for the lack of gas pedals, or this would be a very short trip. Before he climbed in, Bob placed his stuff in the plane and walked around, feeling everything as if he were afraid something might fall off. While he had his nose stuck in the engine, I made like a jaguar—a distant relative of mine—and leaped into the plane. No problem. It was about the same height as a car, with the same type of front seats to hide under.

While he had his nose stuck in the engine, I made like a jaguar—a distant relative of mine—and leaped into the plane.

So, there I was, inside a real airplane. Flying looked like fun, but I was remembering things like, "If God wanted man to fly, He would have given him wings," and "The real problem is getting them off the ground. They always come down again."

I was beginning to have butterflies in my

stomach. Usually, that's okay. I like butterfly, garnished with a little lemongrass. What do you mean "Yuck!"? So, I eat my meat live; you eat yours dead. Stop being picky.

Anyway, Bob was now pretty sure things won't fall off, so he got in the airplane and connected all sorts of wires to things he put over his ears. He put his maps and other stuff on the seat next to him, looked at the dashboard for a while (I think he was trying to figure out how to start the thing), and closed the door. He must have figured it out because he opened the window and yelled, "Clear!" I'm not sure if that meant it was all clear to him, or "Get out of the way, I'm coming through!", but either way, he pulled a couple of levers, turned a key, and everything in the plane just went berserk. There was a roar you won't believe, followed by shaking, rattling, and vibrating. The plane then pitched forward. Man, was it bad. I would have jumped out the other window if my fur hadn't stood up so high on my back that I got stuck under the seat.

Next thing you know, he was talking as calm as could be to someone who wasn't me. "Airport tower, this is five three niner niner five on the apron ready to taxi."

"Niner niner five, wind is 130 at 10; altimeter is 29.7. Taxi to two two and hold."

"Niner niner five to two two and hold, roger."

I had no idea what all that was about, but the noise increased, and I could feel the plane move forward. I guess, since we didn't crash or explode like I thought we were going to, all that commotion was supposed to happen, but sheesh, talk about making a guy nervous and confused. I slipped out from under the seat behind Bob and leaped into the luggage compartment. From there, I could see what was happening without being seen.

Bob drove his plane in between several others that were parked, and he didn't hit one of them. This brought us out to a nice, straight road. We traveled along that for a minute or so, and then Bob made a left turn onto another road. This felt like a trip to the grocery store, except for one thing: the plane didn't steer right. When he turns the car's steering wheel clockwise, the car goes right. When he turns it the other way, the car goes left. But when Bob had the plane's steering wheel turned all the way to the right, the plane went straight along the road. It was also at this time that I noticed he was driving on the wrong side of the road. Well, not exactly the wrong side—he was driving right down the middle, following this big yellow line. Luckily, there was no traffic coming the other way or we would have been in an accident. I would have to remember to talk to him about that later.

We came to another road, a much wider

road, but instead of driving on the road, he turned the airplane to face the grass. I couldn't figure out how he did that until I realized he turned the steering wheel the wrong way again. Sheesh! I thought that would stop him, but no, he jammed his feet hard against the brakes, pushed a lever on the dashboard, and turned several switches. Nothing seemed to happen—except I was scared out of my skin. The plane seemed to have a mind of its own and wanted to jump into the weeds. Before it could, Bob figured out he's facing the wrong way. He slowed the engine and turned the plane in the right direction. No problem.

"Airport Tower, niner niner five ready to take off. Over," Bob said into the radio.

"Niner niner five, hold position, please," came the reply.

So, we sat there. What a drag. The big sky was waiting for us, and the guy on the other end of the radio wouldn't let us take off. He was probably reading the comics or something because he sure wasn't paying attention to us.

WWWHHHAAAMMMOOO!!! I wouldn't have believed it if I hadn't seen it with my own eyes. This humongous green thing with giant wings came kerplunking down, crunching kaboom right in front of us, screaming as it raced down the road like a load of cats caught in a cement mixer. Holy dogs, what a sight.

"Cessna niner niner five, take position and hold. When the C-130 is clear, I'll give you permission."

"Niner niver five, roger that."

Bob pushed a little plug or lever thing, and the plane moved out to a big white line in the middle of the wide road before turning to face the green thing that was almost out of sight by now.

"Niner niner five cleared for take-off. Watch for wake turbulence on the runway."

"Niner niner five rolling," Bob said as he pushed the lever in. The engine roared even louder this time, and the plane rolled down the road. Okay, it's not a road. It's really called a runway, but we pilots want you non-pilots to understand what we're talking about. What? I didn't say runaway, I said runway. You read it wrong. Sheesh! That's why I said "road" in the first place.

We traveled along at a speed that always gets Bob pulled over by the police on the highway, when, all of a sudden, he pulled the steering wheel out of its socket and onto his lap. I ducked behind the seat, but when nothing bad happened, I came back up to look. We weren't on the ground anymore! We were higher than the trees and the buildings—too far up for a cat to land on his feet, that's for sure. And I could see that the big green thing that whooshed past us was a giant airplane as we flew over it. It didn't look so big from up here. In fact, nothing looked so big from up here—there was just a lot more to see.

Although we were almost one-thousand feet above the ground now, it felt like we were driving on a bumpy road. We bounced side to side, then up and down. I began to think this was a bad idea. Cats may have nine lives, but no one ever said we couldn't use them up all at once. That's when I made my presence known to Bob. I leaped up, intending to land on the back seat, but as I jumped, the plane dropped like a rock. Instead of landing on the back seat, I ended up on the floor of the front seat.

"Hi, Spike," Bob said. "Enjoying the flight?"

I realized he knew I was there the whole time.

"When did you find out I was here?" I asked.

"I saw you sneaking into the car back home."

"So, it's okay?"

"I promised you a plane ride, didn't I?" Bob said with a smile.

And that was that. I was getting my plane ride, and I didn't have to go through all that sneaking around to get it. I was so shocked that Bob knew I was here, I forgot I was scared and wanted to get my feet back on the ground—at least until Bob turned the steering wheel and the plane turned hard to the right. Of course, I'm a cat. I was curious. Scared or not, I needed to see what was going on, so I jumped onto the seat so I could look out the window. We were really high now. Bob said five-thousand feet, and the flying was much smoother now. *Not bad,* I thought. *Maybe this flying thing could be fun.*

Of course, I'm a cat. I was curious. Scared
or not, I needed to see what was going on, so I
jumped onto the seat so I could look out the window.

"I expect you're a bit nervous," Bob said.

"Well, let's say I'm concerned. I'm not the

cowering-cat type, but the noise did tingle

my cat feathers a little."

"That's normal, Spike. I expect that you'll

get used to it. The engine is louder than a car engine, but a lot of the noise is from the propeller pushing the air, just like the high-speed fan at home. Once we get to seven-thousand feet, I'll slow the engine down, and it will be quieter. I wear these special earphones to protect my ears from the noise. They were designed to be used in helicopters, which are really noisy. If you decide you like flying, I'll make you a special set. With your acute hearing, you should wear hearing protectors so you don't go deaf."

He pulled out the little knob on the dashboard, and the engine slowed down a little, making it quieter. At the same time, he pushed the steering wheel forward and the plane levelled. "Now, I'll set the controls to let the plane fly itself. All I have to do is check the instruments and make minor adjustments to keep us where we should be."

"You mean the plane flies itself?" I asked, worried again.

"Just about. On a day like today, when the wind is calm, there's not much for a pilot to do."

I held my breath as he took his hand off the steering wheel and his feet off the pedals, then looked out the window, waiting for the plane to race, nose first, toward the ground.

Nothing happened.

"See, the plane is set for straight and

level flight, so unless I, or the wind, or the temperature changes, we'll continue straight and level. Airplanes are designed to fly, right? So, I've learned to leave it alone and let it do what it does best."

"It's that easy?" I said, not sure he wasn't kidding around. I never thought Bob was very funny, so that was the sort of joke he'd tell.

"Sure," he said. "Why don't you take the controls and fly it for awhile?"

"Uh ... I think I'll pass."

"Oh, come on, Spike. I have the same controls on my side. If anything goes wrong, I'll take over. Like you always say, 'No problem.'"

Right, no problem. I reached out with one paw, then a second, and just as they were about to touch the steering wheel, Bob spoke up.

"What, are you crazy? Wait until I explain what all these controls and instruments do. First, I'm the PIC, or pilot in command, which is why I'm in the left seat. You, the passenger, are in the right seat. Now, the most important controls are the yoke—that thing that looks like the steering wheel— the rudder pedals on the floor, and this little black-handled knob on the dashboard. Pull the wheel toward you and you climb. Push it forward and you descend. Turn it and you bank, or tip, the wing and start to turn. When you do this, push a little on one of the rudder pedals to finish the turn. Watch me while I make a right turn."

He turned the wheel—err, yoke— clockwise while he pushed the right pedal with his foot. The right wing dropped, and the plane turned to the right.

"How does that happen?" I asked.

"The rudder is the part of the airplane's tail that acts just like the rudder on a boat." He then turned the yoke in the opposite direction and pushed the left pedal down, bringing the plane back to straight and level. "Watch my feet."

He pushed the right pedal, and then

pushed in the left pedal. The plane's nose turned right, then left, just like a boat.

"Now, watch the wings while I turn the yoke. Do you see the long panel on the outer railing edge?"

As I looked where he said, I saw a panel on the back of the wing raise up. This caused the plane to bank to the right. He turned the wheel in the opposite direction, and the panel went down, banking the plane to the left.

"That's how you steer the plane," Bob said. "Now, watch this."

He pushed the yoke forward, and the nose of the plane dropped, sending us downward. I felt like I was floating in space. He then pulled it back toward his chest, and the nose came up, making me feel like my fur was weighted with rocks.

"How come I felt lighter and heavier when you did that?"

"You spend all your time climbing up and jumping down. You tell me."

"Okay," I said, "when the nose is down, we go down, decreasing the effect of gravity, so I feel lighter. When the nose goes up, we go against gravity, so I feel heavier."

"Right. Smart cat. Now, you try it," Bob said. Noticing my hesitation, he added, "Go ahead. I'll just sit back and enjoy the ride."

I slowly put my paws on the yoke and

pushed it to the right. The right wing dropped slightly, but we didn't seem to be turning much. "I'll add a little right rudder," Bob said, "and we'll make a nice coordinated turn."

He was right, and so I tried making a left. I turned the yoke counterclockwise, Bob pushed the pedal, and we turned left. I pushed; we went down. I pulled ... and pulled myself onto the yoke. My weight pushed to the left until the yoke almost turned upside down. The plane turned over on its side and headed right for the ground. My claws came out, and I hung on for dear life. Bob shot up out of his seat, pulled back on the yoke, and turned it to the right. Gradually, we came back to straight and level flight.

My weight pushed to the left until the yoke
almost turned upside down. The plane turned
over on its side and headed right for the ground.

"What happened?" I asked, wondering if there was a litter box aboard. A turn like that can scare the stuff right out of you.

"I guess you aren't big enough to pull the nose up. When you pulled too hard, you pulled yourself out of the seat. Your weight was on the left, so the yoke turned sharply left, the nose dropped, and you know the rest. Fortunately, planes are pretty sturdy and can handle the abuse."

"You saying I abused your plane?"

"Well, not on purpose. It was more my fault than yours. I should have realized what was going to happen and been quicker to react, too. Sorry about that."

"That was dangerous," I said, a quiver in my voice. "We could have crashed."

"Not much of a chance of crashing at this altitude, but if we were closer to the ground, it would have been very dangerous. That's why we're up so high—to keep us safe from cats."

"Not funny, dipstick." See? I told you I didn't think Bob was very funny. "Let's go home."

"Okay. Take her back to the airport and land her."

"Where's the parachute," I said. "I'm leaving."

"No parachutes," Bob said, "but I'll fly over some trees and you can try your luck. I'm sure you can climb down."

"Stop the chatter and get us down. Then, get me to a litter box real quick."

So, that's how I flew an airplane. Lucky for Bob, I was there. I'm not sure he would have been able to regain control if it hadn't been for my help.

SpikE the Cat and the BurGLar

Afigure emerged from the shadow of the carriage house, and as if floating on a mirrored lake, moved across the lawn and disappeared into the shadow cast by the rear wall of the main house. Anyone watching would have only seen the movement of darkness into darkness, but I'm a cat with much sharper eyes than any human. The figure moved up the column connecting the lower and upper porch. Once on the upper porch, the shadow again became one with the blackness. Noiselessly, he lifted the window sash an imperceptible fraction of an inch.

Wait ... listen ... another movement. Wait ... nothing ... more. Wait ... listen ... nothing ... Finally, enough space to crawl into the room. Then, a brief flash of light, no more than an instant. Seconds later, the shadow reappeared, gliding across the porch and down the column. He then traversed the yard and was gone.

CAT BURGLAR STRIKES AGAIN read the headline in the next day's newspaper.

CAT BURGLAR STRIKES AGAIN read the headline in the next day's newspaper. Now, normally I would object to the term "cat burglar". After all, we cats are maligned enough, but I made an exception for this guy.

Sure, he was a little left of making an honest living, but he knew the cat moves and didn't leave any clues.

Every year, the city of Saratoga Springs has the same problem. The country's oldest racetrack opens for the month of August, bringing people from all over the world to "bet on the ponies." They walk up to a little window at the racetrack, give the guy behind the window a fistful of money, and say something like, "Noodlesnooper to win in the third." For this, they get a cardboard ticket. The horses line up in a cage-like thing in the middle of the track, and when a bell rings, the cage door opens, and some guy yells, "They're off!"

Everybody watching the race starts jumping up and down and yelling for Noodlesnooper to go faster or slower, depending on whether they want him to win or lose. The whole time they're jumping up and down and losing their minds, the horses run like crazy. The riders, known as 'jockeys', whip their horses to run faster. After about a minute, one horse wins the race, and then just about everybody rips up their ticket, gets back in line, and buys another one. Humans. Sheesh! Sometimes there's no point to what they do.

At night, they go out to eat when they have perfectly good food at home. They go to parties with people they barely known, which allows certain other people they don't know, like the cat burglar, to let themselves into their rooms and help themselves to all their money and stuff. The people come back to their rooms, find out they've been robbed, and then jump up and down like they did at the track. I'm not sure what the difference is in how they lose their money, but when they get robbed, they call the cops. The cops come and investigate. They ask a lot of questions, mess up your room, and dust for fingerprints. The first time I saw them do that, I thought they were killing fleas because they use the same kind of stuff Bob uses on me.

NAME	ADDRESS	ROBBED
Guildersnoggle	Nelson Ave	X
Puffersouff	Union St	X
Goldbangle	Circular St	
Silverspangle	Spring St	
Emeraldgaud	Maple St	
Weatherby	Travers Alley	X
Hoity-Toit	Caroline St	

The cops are pretty smart, though. They usually know who's in town, and like Santa Claus, they know who's been naughty or nice. Sometimes it's pretty simple. They just go down their list of names and visit the people on the naughty list. They find the loot, take the guy away, and that's that. Now, if you know any cops, they'll tell you it isn't that simple, and they're right, particularly when they're up against a real pro like the cat burglar I caught.

Oh, I didn't mention that I caught him? Well, I did.

A few days after the cat burglar broke into the house at the beginning of this story, Bob and Sue invited a few friends into their home. It just so happened that one of them was a cop working on the cat burglar case. Charley and I listened in.

Charley bugged the dining room table with his Super Agent Spy Catching Kit, then he and I slipped away to his bedroom to listen in. Sergeant Cheshire, the cop, explained that they were trying to discover a pattern to the burglaries. They were sure that the same guy was doing all the robberies, but since he left no clues, it was hard to tell. Still, they figured he'd keep busy, and then they would catch him. Sergeant Cheshire explained that the guy only broke in at night, and he knew which people wouldn't be at home because they'd be attending big parties in town.

Charley bugged the dining room table with
his Super Agent Spy Catching Kit, then he and
I slipped away to his bedroom to listen in.

Charley and I snuck down the back hallway

where we kept the old newspapers and found

the society page. We found articles about

the night the Guildersnoggles were robbed,

and the night the Puffersnuffs were robbed,

too. There was a long list of names of people

who attended the parties, but only seven people were at both. For the next few days, we read the society page looking for news of another party. On Friday, we hit pay dirt.

Mr. and Mrs. Goldbangle had invited "a few of their closest and dearest friends" to view slides of their recent vacation to the Sahara Desert. Among those who'd be there were the Guildersnoggles and the Puffersnuffs, as well as the Silverspangles, the Emeraldgauds, the Weatherbys, the Hoity-Toits, and a few others. Fortunately for Charley and me, the party was being held only a few blocks from here. In fact, all the robberies were pretty close to our neighborhood. (It suddenly occurred to me that Bob might be richer than I thought, and I should definitely ask him for better food: you know, real liver and tuna and not the stuff out of a can. I mean, what self-respecting cat would eat that kind of food when his owner lives in this kind of neighborhood?)

Anyway, back to the story. Maybe the neighborhood was part of the pattern. We had to find out where the seven people who attended the other two parties lived. Charley googled their addresses. While all of them lived in Saratoga, only the Emeraldgauds lived here year 'round. The rest rented homes for the track season. But before Charley and I could come up with any more clues, or a way to stop this cat burglar, he struck again. The Weatherbys' home was robbed while they were at the Goldbangles' party. Another couple off the list. This was looking good. Three of the seven people on our list had now been robbed. Assuming the people who got robbed weren't also the cat burglar, we only had to figure out which of the four remaining names it could be.

Charley made a chart that looked like this:

Name	Address	Robbed
Guildersnoggle	Nelson Ave.	X
Puffersnuff	Union St.	X
Goldbangle	Circular St.	
Silverspangle	Spring St.	
Emeraldgaud	Maple St.	
Weatherby	Travers Alley	X
Hoity-Toit	Caroline St.	

On Tuesday, the society page reported that the Puffersnuffs were having a party, and guess what? The other six families were all invited. The party would be held the next night, and sure as kittens, Thursday's paper reported the cat burglar struck again. This time, the Silverspangles had a lighter load to carry home. Now, only three couples hadn't been robbed.

Friday. The morning paper mentioned the Emeraldgauds were having a party, and five of the six would be attending. The Goldbangles were going home early. Still, this meant that two families who hadn't been robbed yet would be there, and one of them was throwing the party. Maybe the Hoity-Toits were next.

Charley had a Cub Pack meeting to attend, so I hustled over to Caroline Street to watch the Hoity-Toits' house. I found a nice tree limb above the garbage cans, so at least I could have dinner while I waited. Sure, it was leftovers, but when you're on a stakeout, you eat what you can. I got lucky—someone had fish for dinner that night. I jumped down to get the lid off the can when I spotted this guy: all in black, wearing a black hood and black gloves. Figures. I'm about to enjoy a fish dinner when the cat burglar shows up. Sheesh, the sacrifices you make to do detective work. Still, it was worth it. I was about to become a hero. Me, a talking cat, would become a hero in the human world. Go figure!

Instead of gliding across the yard from shadow to shadow, she walked around the swimming pool, which was right next to the two-storied back porch. Since we cats have super-terrific night vision, I could see her plain as day. Did you notice I said she? Right. The burglar was a woman. How could I tell? Her sweater was tight-fitting; her pants were tight-fitting. If that was a man, he had problems.

She went through the door—which wasn't even locked—and headed up the stairs to the second-floor hallway. I slipped in behind her before the door closed. She walked to one of the bedrooms that opened onto the porch. Opening a dresser drawer on the other side of the room, she took out a box, opened it, removed all the jewels, and dropped them into a black bag. She stepped through the open, sliding-glass door to the porch to see if the coast was clear. Well, it may have been clear outside, but I was right on her heels.

Suddenly, she stepped back. Now, as far as cats go, I'm pretty careful, but how was I supposed to know she would go backwards? Squash! Right on the old tail. "MEEOWWW!" says I, as I attached myself to her leg.

Squash! Right on the old tail. "MEEOWWW!"
says I, as I attached myself to her leg.

"YEEOWWW!" says she as she took a leap. Unfortunately for her, she was pointing toward the railing. Without warning, she flipped over the railing and plunged, with me attached, through the air and straight into the swimming pool.

"LEMEEOWWWT of here!" says I, not liking water one bit. Lights switched on all over the place. I swam to the edge of the pool, pulled my soaking-wet fur onto dry concrete, and shagged on out of there. Hero-schmero! I wasn't sticking around for any reward. I was wet, and as we all know, cats don't like wet. I was off to a drier climate, like home. After all, it was only a few blocks away. When I got home, I shook off the remaining water, got myself together, and as poised as I could manage with wet fur clinging to my body, slipped through the cat door, found my bed, and went to sleep.

In the morning, as usual, Sue had my breakfast ready. It may not have been a hero's feast, but I ate it all. After last night's adventure, I was too hungry for any finicky business. Bob said "Good morning," to me, but my mouth was too full of liver pate and whitefish to respond, so he then pretended to read the newspaper to Sue. "Look at this: CAT BURGLAR CAPTURED," he said, pointing to a big picture on the front page. "Last night, police fished the alleged burglar, identified as Mrs. Helen Hoity-Toit, from a pool located at the reported scene of the crime. Mrs. Hoity-Toit, dressed all in black, including black ski mask and gloves, claimed she was merely taking a moonlight swim after a stressful day at the track, but upon investigation, officers on the scene found a bag of imitation jewels at the bottom of the pool. A search of the alleged burglar's home produced a suitcase full of items reported missing following a rash of recent burglaries plaguing Saratoga Springs. Police picked up Mr. Harry Hoity-Toit at a nearby party. Both are currently being held at the city lock-up for further questioning. Officers believe Mrs. Hoity-Toit was robbing her own apartment to remove suspicion from herself and her husband. The Hoity-Toits are believed to be the infamous cat burglar team of Monte-en-Pair, who have, until recently, confined themselves to the French Riviera."

Sheesh! No mention of me, at all. Sure, the

police did a good job investigating the crime after I gave them the burglar! Oh, well. What can you do? Humans, right?

I gave Charley a big, knowing wink, and he smiled back, knowing who the real hero was last night. Me, Spike the Cat.

Printed in the United States
By Bookmasters